For Dad, with love —D.U.

For Ade, Nathan, Elia & Keziah —H.M.

Dial Books for Young Readers
Penguin Young Readers Group
An imprint of Penguin Random House LLC
375 Hudson Street
New York, NY 10014

Printed in China
ISBN 9780735228504

10 9 8 7 6 5 4 3 2 1

Design by Jennifer Kelly | Text set in Gotham
and hand-lettered by Hannah Marks

The artwork was created digitally with Photoshop.

THE PANDA PROBLEM

by DEBORAH UNDERWOOD

illustrated by HANNAH MARKS

Dial Books for Young Readers

Once upon a time, there was a panda who lived in a beautiful bamboo grove.

But the panda had a BIG problem.

Excuse me?

Psssst . . . this is a story!
I'm the narrator.
And YOU are the main character.

The main character? That sounds important!

It is!
But you need a
problem.

Why?

So you can *solve*
the problem.

That's how stories work.

Do you wish you could fly?

Nope.

Do you wish you were green?

Nope!

Is your paw sore?

Oh! Let me check...

Nope!

HOW AM I SUPPOSED TO TELL A STORY
IF YOU DON'T HAVE A PROBLEM?

You're right.
How could a sweet
little panda like me
be a problem?
Unless...

Hey! Where did you get that?

You are definitely starting to feel
like a problem.

Next time I am going to narrate a book about rocks.
Nice, quiet rocks.

Aliens?! There's no such thing as . . .

Hi, aliens.

But the setting for this story is a bamboo grove!
There are no penguins in bamboo groves!

Well . . . sometimes the problem gets worse.
But that won't happen now.
BECAUSE THINGS CAN'T *GET* ANY WORSE!

GLUG GLUG

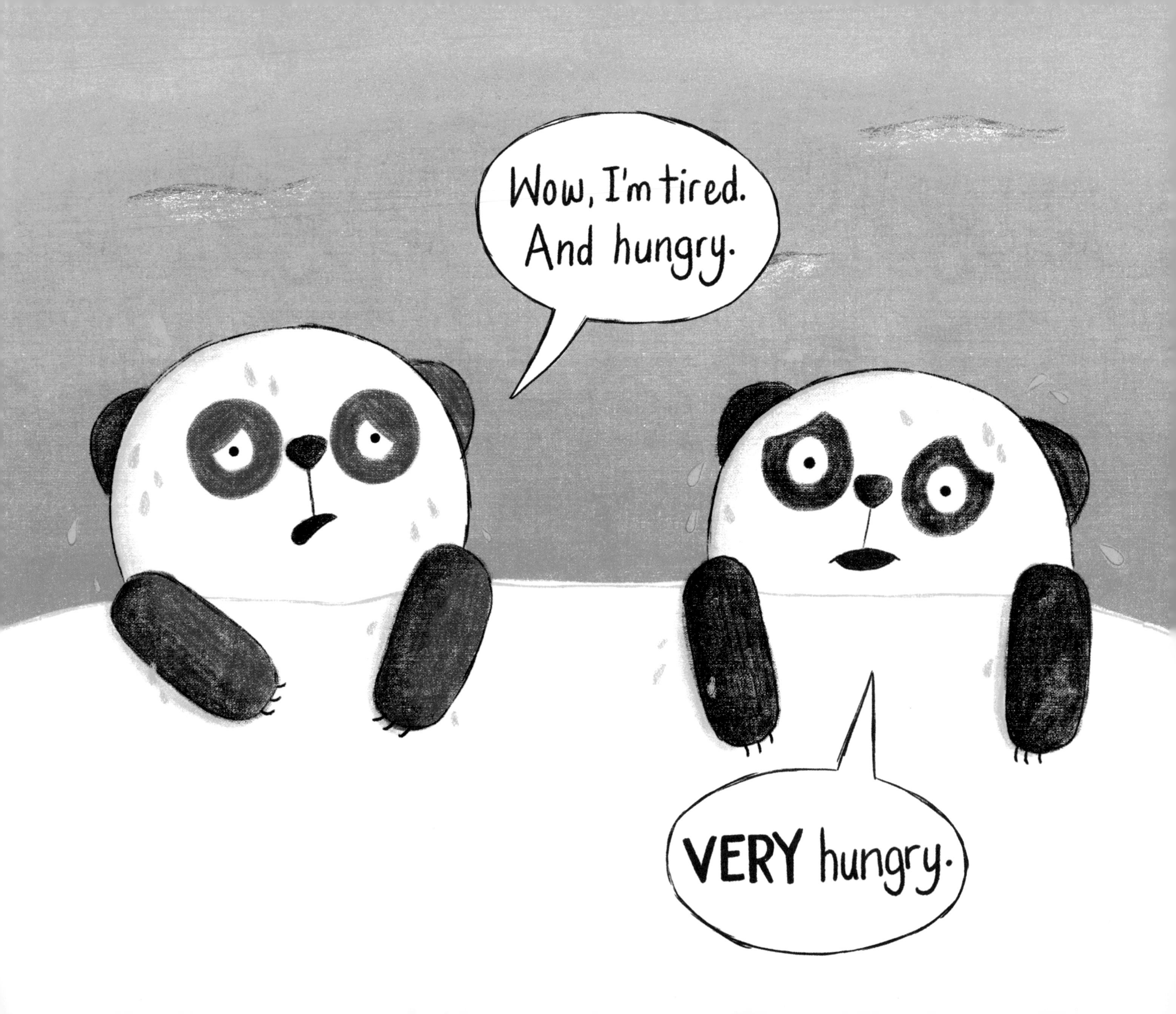
Wow, I'm tired. And hungry.
VERY hungry.

Well, well. That *is* a problem.
How will you solve it?

Okay, Narrator. If you get us home, we will stop making problems and help you tell **YOUR** panda story! No banjos. No burping. No penguins.

Really? Well . . . all right.

Ahem.

Together the pandas and aliens came up with a great plan!

The pandas and aliens spelled out "HELP!" with jelly beans.

The aliens' ship scooped everyone up
in its tractor beam . . .

. . . and dropped them safely back in the bamboo grove, where everyone settled down to a bamboo and jelly bean feast!

That's okay. Let's try again tomorrow.
I'm sleepy too.

Hey—why don't you tell ME a bedtime story?

Nope.